Note to parents, carers and teachers

Read it yourself is a series of modern stories, favourite characters and traditional tales written in a simple way for children who are learning to read. The books can be read independently or as part of a guided reading session.

Each book is carefully structured to include many high-frequency words vital for first reading. The sentences on each page are supported closely by pictures to help with understanding, and to offer lively details to talk about.

The books are graded into four levels that progressively introduce wider vocabulary and longer stories as a reader's ability and confidence grows.

Ideas for use

- Begin by looking through the book and talking about the pictures. Has your child heard this story before?

- Help your child with any words he does not know, either by helping him to sound them out or supplying them yourself.

- Developing readers can be concentrating so hard on the words that they sometimes don't fully grasp the meaning of what they're reading. Answering the puzzle questions on pages 30 and 31 will help with understanding.

For more information and advice on Read it yourself and book banding, visit **www.ladybird.com/readityourself**

Book
Band
7

Level 2 is ideal for children who have received some reading instruction and can read short, simple sentences with help.

Special features:

Frequent repetition of main story words and phrases

Short, simple sentences

Little Red Riding Hood lived with her mother and father in a house in the forest.

6

Large, clear type

Careful match between story and pictures

Little Red Riding Hood's father was in the forest.

He ran to Grandmother's house to help.

26

27

Educational Consultant: Geraldine Taylor
Book Banding Consultant: Kate Ruttle

A catalogue record for this book is available from the British Library

Published by Ladybird Books Ltd
80 Strand, London, WC2R 0RL
A Penguin Company

005

ISBN: 978-0-72327-290-8

Printed in China

Little Red
Riding Hood

Illustrated by Diana Mayo

Little Red Riding Hood
lived with her mother
and father in a house
in the forest.

One day, Little Red Riding Hood's mother said, "Will you take these cakes to Grandmother?"

"Yes," said Little Red Riding Hood, and off she went.

Grandmother's house was on the other side of the forest. A wolf lived in the forest.

When the wolf saw Little
Red Riding Hood he said,
"I will eat her all up!"
He ran to Grandmother's
house.

Little Red Riding Hood
knocked on her
grandmother's door.

"Come in," said
a funny voice.

Little Red Riding Hood
went in the house.

"Come closer, my dear,"
said the funny voice.

"Oh, Grandmother," said Little Red Riding Hood. "What big ears you have!"

"All the better to hear you with, my dear," said the funny voice. "Come closer."

19

"Oh, Grandmother," said
Little Red Riding Hood.
"What big eyes you have!"

"All the better to see
you with, my dear,"
said the funny voice.
"Come closer."

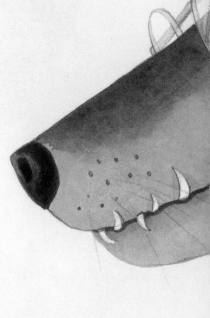

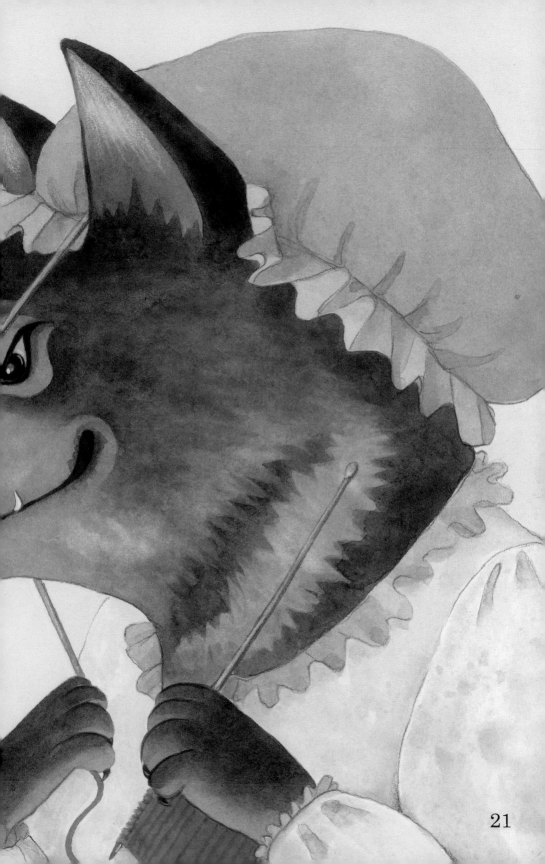

21

"Oh, Grandmother," said Little Red Riding Hood. "What big teeth you have!"

"All the better to eat you with!" cried the wolf.

The wolf jumped up
and chased Little Red
Riding Hood round and
round the house.

"Help!" cried Little Red
Riding Hood.

Little Red Riding Hood's father was in the forest.

He ran to Grandmother's house to help.

The wolf jumped up when he saw Little Red Riding Hood's father.

Then he ran and ran and was never seen in the forest again.

How much do you remember about the story of Little Red Riding Hood? Answer these questions and find out!

- **Where is Little Red Riding Hood going?**

- **Who sees her in the forest?**

- **Who is the wolf pretending to be?**

- **Who rescues Little Red Riding Hood and Grandmother?**

Look at the pictures and match them to the story words.

Grandmother

Little Red Riding Hood

forest

wolf

father

Read it yourself with Ladybird

Tick the books you've read!

For beginner readers who can read short, simple sentences with help.

Level 2

 Beauty and the Beast ☐

 Chicken Licken ☐

 Little Red Riding Hood ☐

 Nature Trail ☐

 Sports Day ☐

 Pirate School ☐

 Rumpelstiltskin ☐

 Sleeping Beauty ☐

 The Gingerbread Man ☐

 Sly Fox and Red Hen ☐

 The Tale of Jemima Puddle-Duck ☐

 The Three Little Pigs ☐

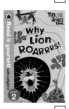 Why Lion ROARRRS! ☐

 Topsy and Tim The Big Race ☐

 Town Mouse and Country Mouse ☐

 Dan's Dragon ☐

For more confident readers who can read simple stories with help.

Level 3

 YOU won't like this present as much as I DO! ☐

 The Elves and the Shoemaker ☐

 Hansel and Gretel ☐

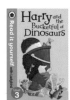 Harry and the Bucketful of Dinosaurs ☐

 Jack and the Beanstalk ☐

 Furi on Music Island ☐

 Poppet Stows Away ☐

 Rapunzel ☐

 The Red Knight ☐

Available on the App Store

The Read it yourself with Ladybird app is now available for iPad, iPhone and iPod touch

App also available on Android devices